Bubbly & Billionaires

The Boozy Book Club Series

By

Rose Bak

AF613024

BUBBLY & BILLIONAIRES

© 2022 by Rose Bak

ALL RIGHTS RESERVED. No portion of this book may be reproduced, transmitted, downloaded, decompiled, reverse engineered, or stored in or introduced into any information storage retrieval system in any form by any means without express permission from the publisher, except as permitted by U.S. copyright law. For permissions contact: Rosebakenterprises@msn.com

Table of Contents

About This Book 1
Dedication 2
Prologue – Emma 3
Wyatt 5
Emma 10
Wyatt 15
Emma 20
Wyatt 25
Emma 30
Wyatt 36
Emma 40
Wyatt 45
Emma 50
Wyatt 55
Emma 60
Epilogue – Emma 64
Special Preview 67
Other Books by Rose Bak 71
About the Author 73

About This Book

Falling in love with billionaires is only something that happens in romance books, right?

Nurse Emma Edwards is known for her bedside manner. Her quiet confidence and a sunny personality can cheer up even the grumpiest patient.

But her latest patient isn't just grumpy, he's successful, rich, and incredibly handsome. Wyatt Simmons made a fortune in business, but the widower is also quite lonely – at least until his daughter insists on hiring a nurse to care for him after emergency surgery. He might not want a nurse, but he does want Emma – for the rest of his life.

They come from different worlds, but they're both old enough to know what they want – love.

"Bubbly & Billionaires" is book one in the "Boozy Book Club" series. Each story in the series is a steamy standalone featuring a couple in their fifties, a nosy group of book club friends, matchmaking family members, and a sweet happily ever after that proves anyone can find love later in life.

Download this instalove romantic comedy today!

This book includes a special excerpt from "Until You Came Along", book one of the Oliver Boys Band series, available now from all major online retailers.

Be sure to join Rose's mailing list and get a free book. Click here[1] to be the first to hear about all the latest releases and special sales.

1. https://storyoriginapp.com/giveaways/62ee758e-068f-11eb-904e-c373f6014fe1

Dedication

For all the billionaire romance fans.

Prologue – Emma

Two weeks ago...

"Good evening ladies, and welcome to the Boozy Book Club. For those of you who don't know me, my name is Evie Fontenot and I'm the owner of Boozy Books."

The group clapped politely. I looked around and saw a couple of new faces. Evie's Boozy Book Club was really taking off. What started off as just our group of five friends now had grown to over a dozen members.

My friend Evie was a genius. After an unexpected divorce left her with nothing, she had crowd-funded the down payment to purchase a popular bookstore downtown. When the original owners announced that they were retiring due to unexpected health complications, they'd been thrilled to give one of their best customer and a fellow book lover a good deal on the store.

First she had cleaned up the store, opening up space, adding seating, and improving the lighting. When she was done with that, Evie had turned the meeting rooms upstairs into a little café that served coffee, wine, beer, pastries, and sandwiches. We'd all helped her knock down the walls and do some of the pre-work on the café, working out our stress with sledgehammers. That had been a fun day.

Evie renamed the store Boozy Books and had a huge grand reopening. Since then, business had been going better than she ever could have hoped. Everyone in town loved the idea of having a coffee or an adult beverage while reading and shopping for books. Boozy Books was also a popular place for someone going on a first date or tackling an afternoon of teleworking.

Last year Evie had introduced the Boozy Book Club. The concept was simple: every month one member was responsible for picking the book for the next meeting, as well as a signature cocktail that would be served during the meeting. Book club members were charged a small fee to cover the cost of the refreshments, and since most of them purchased the book of the month from Boozy Books, it also helped with sales.

We had just finished discussing the book of the month, a collection of feminist poetry, and we were all enjoying a glass of Pimms, a gin-based liqueur. I'd never had it before, but it was delicious. I would definitely order it again sometime.

"I hope you all enjoyed our Pimms and Poetry night," Evie continued. "Our next selection is brought to us by one of our founding book club members, Rachael. Rachael, please share next month's theme."

My friend Rachael stood up from her seat in the row in front of me. "OK ladies, I have a special treat for you. The theme for next month is 'Bubbly and Billionaires'. We'll be reading 'The Billionaire's Curvy Assistant' and for our discussion, the drink of the night will be Champagne Cocktails."

The book club members clapped politely. Although the group read a variety of book genres, romantic fiction was always a popular choice with the ladies.

"Thank you Rachael. Copies of the book are available to purchase at the registers downstairs. Enjoy your evening."

"I hate billionaire stories," I grumbled to Dawn. She and Evie and I were all best friends.

"Why?" she asked curiously.

"They're so unrealistic," I grumbled. "What's wrong with your run-of-the-mill millionaires? At least those are more common. I mean, what are there, like a couple of hundred billionaires in the world?"

Dawn laughed. "I think there's a few more than that."

"Even if there are, billionaires don't fall in love with working class girls like us."

Lainie giggled. "I'd hardly call you working class Emma. You make pretty good money as a nurse."

"Maybe so, but you don't run into a lot of billionaires in everyday life. Where would you even meet someone like that?"

Wyatt

"I don't need a damn nurse! I'm not an invalid."

"Dad, you just had surgery and walked out of the hospital before they released you. Since you didn't stay in the hospital like your doctor advised, you're damn well going to have a nurse to keep an eye on you until you've recovered."

My daughter Susannah tucked the blankets around me and pressed a kiss on the top of my head like I was a toddler. Damn hospital. I'd had my appendix removed yesterday and after one night of everyone hovering around me and taking my damn temperature every five minutes I couldn't take it anymore. I'd walked right out at five in the morning and called my car service to take me back to my home.

My normally peaceful and quiet home. Or it was until the hospital called my daughter and tattled on me. She was listed as my emergency contact and she'd high-tailed it over to my house to read me the riot act. Susannah was a fixer. Within ninety minutes of her arrival, she'd moved me into the downstairs guest room, made me breakfast, ordered groceries, and hired me a damn nurse.

I sighed. I loved my daughter, really I did, but I just wanted to recover in peace.

"I'm fine, I just need to sleep," I told her. "You can't any sleep in that damn hospital."

I was in a bit of pain, not that I would admit that to Susannah. I shifted to reach for my water bottle and before I could stop myself, I grimaced at the pull of pain from my stitches.

"See?" she said. "You do need help. Now quit being such a grump and let me take care of you for once."

Susannah and I had always been close, but since her mother died of breast cancer at only thirty-seven years old, it had been me and my daughter against the world. Susannah was the best of both of us. She'd gotten her keen mind and love of reading from me, but she was also social and thoughtful like her mother. It's what had made my wife and me such a good match. If it'd been up to me, I'd be a hermit. My wife had forced me to interact with people outside of work and if I was honest, it had been good for me.

The doorbell rang and Susannah hustled off to answer it. I heard her whispering in the hallway, presumably telling the nurse about my injuries, and warning her that I was a grouchy asshole.

Susannah returned a few minutes later with a woman wearing light green scrubs with a pattern of yellow and white daisies. She was tall, towering over my five foot four daughter. My eyes caught on the woman's dark green clogs, before traveling up sturdy legs, curvy hips, a tucked in waist, and generous breasts that were evident even beneath the loose and unflattering scrubs. She wasn't fat or thin, just lush and curvy like a woman should be.

Continuing my perusal, I noted a sharp chin, glossy pink lips, pale white skin with a smattering of freckles across the bridge of her nose, brown eyes, and dark blonde hair that was pulled up into one of those messy buns that women liked to wear. Tendrils of blonde hair escaped and curled down to the top of her shoulders, softening the look. I'd guess she was in her late forties or early fifties, around the same age as me.

My eyes locked onto hers and held. I felt a jolt of awareness race through my body, and judging by the widening of her eyes, she felt it too. *Mine.* Something deep in my soul laid claim to this stranger in the ridiculous flowered scrubs and in that moment, I knew I was fucked.

The woman visibly shook herself, breaking the spell between us. She hustled forward, holding out her hand and giving me a cheerful smile.

"Hello Mr. Simmons, my name is Emma Edwards. I'll be taking care of you for the next few days."

"I don't need any help," I grumbled even as I took her hand. It felt soft and small in mine, and I wanted to never let her go. I could feel the unexpected connection between us. I suspected Emma could feel it too. She pulled her hand away quickly, as if she'd been burned.

What on Earth was wrong with me? I didn't like strangers, and I sure as hell didn't want to fall in love with someone new. My wife and I had a good life together, and I'd loved her dearly. After watching her slip into a long, agonizing death I'd promised myself that I was done. No more dating. No more love. It was the only way to protect myself from the pain.

But that all went out the window the minute the woman took my hand. Plans changed.

"He refuses to take any pain meds," Susannah tattled on me, seemingly oblivious to the tension between me and Emma.

"Well let me take a quick look at that wound," Emma said, giving me a big, cheerful smile. I had a feeling she was one of those happy sunshiney people, unlike me.

The nurse stepped into the en-suite bathroom, and I heard the water running as she washed her hands. She returned a minute later and without asking, slid the blanket down to my waist. I was wearing a pajama top that I'd left open to keep the pressure of the fabric off my throbbing wound. The incisions hurt more than I had expected, given their small size.

Emma carefully removed the gauze bandage, tossing it into the garbage can near the bed, and leaned down to get a closer look at the incision. I studied the top of her head while she studied my abdomen. On instinct, I started to suck in my gut, but that caused more pain than I wanted to deal with. Fortunately, I was in pretty good shape for an old man. I ran most days and lifted weights three times a week. Just because I was fifty-three, that was no reason to let myself go entirely.

"Can you hand me my bag please Susannah?" Emma asked with another happy smile.

My daughter picked up her medical backpack and Emma slid the zipper open. Finding a pair of latex gloves, she covered her hands and then probed around the incision site gently. I hissed in pain, and she looked up at me under her lashes.

"You're going to take your pain meds," she ordered sternly as she covered the wound with a fresh gauze bandage.

I shivered at her tone and willed myself not to get a hard-on. Stern Emma was even sexier than happy Emma.

"I don't like those damn things," I replied sullenly. I heard Susannah sigh deeply behind us.

"Too bad," Emma said, still with that stern tone. "Your body can't heal properly if it's busy fighting the pain. You will take your pain meds today, and we'll re-evaluate again in a day or two with the goal of stepping down to ibuprofen."

Without being asked, Susannah handed her the bottle of pills she'd somehow procured after I left the hospital. I swear my daughter could manage the most complex operations like a seasoned military general. Her time was wasted in her social services job. She should be running a small country or something.

Emma glanced at the label, then asked, "Are you taking any other medication?"

"Just my cholesterol medication."

She nodded. "Great, that won't interfere with these."

She smiled again and I caught my breath. She really was quite beautiful. *Mine.* I heard the word deep in my soul.

Emma poured two tablets onto her gloved palm and moved it closer to me. When I didn't take the pills, she grabbed my chin firmly between the fingers of her other hand, pulling my mouth open.

"Hey!" I protested.

The sneaky woman used the opportunity to toss the pills into my mouth, then she handed me the water bottle. I glared at her but took a long swallow to wash down the chalky pills. I ran one of the largest companies in the country and I'd just been outmaneuvered by a curvy little sunshine in daisy scrubs.

"Wow," Susannah said, clearly impressed. "You're good."

"You've got to throw them towards the back of the throat, like how you do with a dog," Emma said cheerfully.

I gave her my best scowl, the one that made most of my employees cower, but Emma was unaffected.

"Well Dad, I guess I'm leaving you in capable hands," Susannah announced. She leaned over the bed and gave me a kiss on the cheek. "You be good," she whispered in my ear.

She turned her attention back to Emma. "Thanks for your help Ms. Edwards. I should be back here around seven o'clock if that works for you. As I mentioned, there's lunch for both of you in the fridge, you just need to heat it up when you get hungry. When I come back I'll bring dinner for Dad."

"That sounds fine Susannah thank you," Emma replied. "And please call me Emma."

Susannah looked between the two of us, then hightailed it out of the room, leaving us alone.

"What do we do now?" I grumbled, crossing my arms over my chest, and looking at Emma.

Emma gave me a smile. "Now you rest."

"I'm not tired, damn it."

Ten minutes later, I was fast asleep.

Emma

I watched my patient until he was sound asleep, then slipped out of the room to look around a bit. Susannah had told me I should feel free to eat or drink whatever I wanted, to use any room, and to make myself at home.

As if I could make myself at home in this ginormous mansion. I swear when Susannah had shown me around the main floor earlier, I felt like I was channeling that hillbilly family who moved to Beverly Hills on that show I used to watch when I was a kid.

I'd only seen the downstairs, but the place was full of huge rooms, high-end furniture, and the best of everything, including a media room that looked like it cost more than my house. The house was surprisingly warm though, with comfortable furnishings, colorful throw rugs, family pictures, and enough clutter to look lived in. It all looked expensive, but not obnoxiously so. Large windows helped the space feel light and airy.

My favorite room was the library, where overstuffed furniture was grouped around a large stone fireplace, and packed bookshelves covered two full walls. Clearly my patient loved to read as much as I did. Or someone in the house did, anyway.

Wandering into the kitchen, I found the coffee maker and some coffee pods, and brewed myself a cup of caffeine. I looked out the window as I waited, noting the well landscaped yard which included a giant pool, what I guessed was a pool house, and an impressive view of the ocean in the distance. The house was situated on a cliff over the ocean and separated by neighbors by at least a quarter of an acre on each side. That and the large stone fence gave the house a private feel.

I wasn't sure what Wyatt did for a living, but he must make good money. I'd never known anyone who lived in oceanfront mansion before.

When my coffee was done I settled at the kitchen table to do some work. I figured that Wyatt would probably sleep for a few hours thanks to his pain pills, but the kitchen was close enough that if he called for me I would hear him.

Opening my laptop, I logged onto the Electronic Medical Record system and reviewed Wyatt's file. Fifty-three year old man presented at the Emergency Department with severe stomach pain on the right side and a fever. Upon examination, it was determined that he had a hot appendix and was rushed into surgery before it could burst. Laparoscopic surgery went well, with no complications.

The patient had gotten agitated and demanded to go home while in the recovery room, so the nurses had asked his daughter to intervene. Susannah convinced him to stay overnight, but after an early morning visit from his doctor where the doctor advised staying at the hospital for another twenty-four hours as a precaution, Wyatt checked himself out AMA – against medical advice. The nurses then called his emergency contact, Susannah, to alert her that her father had left. The hospital had made arrangements for Wyatt's pain medication to be filled at their local pharmacy, and recommended that Susannah call an agency and arrange for a home nurse to check on Wyatt.

I noted that Wyatt was generally very healthy, and except to refill his cholesterol medication he rarely visited his primary care doctor. I wasn't surprised; he seemed pretty stubborn.

Stubborn but handsome...

My mind flashed back to meeting my new patient. I'd been a nurse for almost thirty years and never in my life, not once, did I ever have such an intense physical reaction to a patient. When our eyes had met for the first time, it felt like my heart stopped. I'd suddenly had visions of the two of us together in ways that were not appropriate for a nurse and patient relationship—at least outside of those dirty movies my husband used to watch.

He was a good looking man, a "silver fox" my friends would call him. His thick hair used to be dark but was now mostly silver and grey. He had a short grey beard and a mustache that was still mostly brown. His white skin was tanned, as if he spent a lot of time outside and his brown eyes and thin lips were both bracketed by small lines.

When I'd pulled his shirt open to examine his wound I'd been surprised by how fit he was. For a guy his age, he was in good physical shape, with defined pecs and a flat abdomen that spoke of a lifetime of regular workouts.

Curious about my mysterious patient, I did what any nosy person would do – I googled him. Wyatt Simmons was a self-made billionaire. When he was still in college he'd created Simmons Gaming and grown it from a company that sold one war-themed video game to one of the largest privately-held gaming companies in the world. He'd married his college sweetheart Maria, and they'd been seemingly happy until she died ten years ago after a lengthy battle with breast cancer. They had one daughter, Susannah.

There was something so appealing about Wyatt, even with him being such a grouch. If I was looking for a man, and he wasn't my patient, and he wasn't some out-of-my-league billionaire I'd totally go for him. I chuckled to myself as I thought of all the ways he and I weren't a match, as if he would even see me that way. A guy like that dated thirty-year-old girls with big boobs and tiny waists, not a middle aged curvy mother of adult children.

Shaking my head, I closed the computer and picked up my e-reader to dive into our book club selection, 'The Billionaire's Curvy Assistant'. As much as I had grumbled about this month's selection, I was really getting into the story. The billionaire had just confessed his feelings for his much younger curvy assistant, Natasha, and a passionate kiss ensued. Unfortunately, the assistant was now telling her boss that they needed to keep things professional to protect her career. Smart girl. I resolved to follow Natasha's example.

I checked on my patient every twenty minutes or so, and when I popped into his room just after one o'clock I saw that he was waking up. He looked delightfully rumpled and grumpy.

"Good morning," I said cheerfully.

He glanced at the cell phone on the bedside table. "Afternoon you mean. I slept half the day away."

"You need to rest."

"What I need is to take a leak and brush my teeth," he retorted in that grumpy tone. He was adorable.

Against his objections, I insisted on walking with him to the bathroom, before stepping out of the room to give him some privacy.

"Just give me a holler if you need help," I told him.

"I've been peeing on my own since I was a toddler," he grumbled. "I don't need anyone to hold my dick for me."

I stood on the other side of the bathroom door, trying very hard not to imagine myself holding Wyatt's dick. If it was proportionate to the rest of him, it would more than a handful. My nipples tightened at the thought.

I heard Wyatt washing up, followed by the sound of him brushing his teeth. When he stepped back out of the bathroom, he looked a little better. Sometimes cleaning up made a big difference in how a patient felt.

"Are you hungry?" I asked.

"I could eat," he responded, still sounding grumpy. "But you're a nurse, not my maid."

I laughed, appreciating him respecting my role. That wasn't true for many of my private patients.

"It's OK. It's not unusual for me to help with meals on these kind of assignments. Susannah left us some prepared food for our lunch. I just need to heat it up."

"When in the hell did she do everything?" he mused. "She was here less than ninety minutes after I left the hospital."

"Your daughter is a powerhouse, that's for sure."

I settled Wyatt back into bed, pulling the pillows up behind him so he could sit up and lean against the headboard while I heated up our lunch. When I reached across him, my arm connected with his shoulder and we both caught our breath. I turned, my face close enough to him that I could smell the mint of his toothpaste, and whispered, "Sorry."

We stared at each other for several long seconds before I remembered myself and pulled away.

"I'll be back with lunch," I promised, my voice sounding unusually breathy.

As I bustled around the kitchen making a tray for Wyatt I couldn't help but wonder what the hell was wrong me, acting this way around a patient.

Wyatt

I stared at Emma from under my eyelashes while I picked at the food on my tray. I'm sure that wherever Susannah got this food from it was good, but I couldn't concentrate on eating right now. Not when my life was changing so dramatically.

Emma sat in the armchair in one corner of the room, her plate balanced in her lap as she ate the chicken with rice and vegetables. She reached over to grab her water bottle. The movement pulled her scrubs top tighter across her chest, and my dick twitched as I saw the outline of her erect nipples visible through the light fabric.

I never even dreamed that I'd get a second chance at love, but apparently the gods were smiling on me.

I'd been married to my wife for twenty years, and watched her die a long, slow death from uterine cancer. We'd met in college and become fast friends, before our feelings had turned romantic. We'd had a good life together, and I'd loved her as much the day she died as I did the day we got married. But our love had been comfortable, not this instant pull like I felt with Emma.

After I lost her, I figured that was it for me. I'd had my chance at love. Other than the occasional dinners and brief hook-ups to scratch an itch, I hadn't dated anyone seriously in the ten years since Maria had passed away.

But now, looking at Emma, I saw my future. She was so beautiful, so vibrant, so alluring. As much as I cursed the appendicitis that had put me in this situation, I was grateful that it had brought Emma into my life. She wouldn't be leaving it again, that's for sure. She just didn't know it yet. I wasn't a man prone to flights of fancy, and even on my best day I was a grouchy asshole. I liked being alone and before today I would have scoffed at the idea of falling in love at my age, especially with a woman I'd just met. But not anymore.

“How does this traveling nurse gig of yours work?” I asked, breaking the silence.

Emma looked up with one of her cheerful smiles. “I work for on-call for the agency,” she explained. "If they have a short-term assignment that fits my qualifications they offer me the job. Sometimes my assignment is just for a single day, sometimes for a couple of weeks. I pick up a lot of shifts at the hospital and the nursing home, as well as the occasional private client.”

“Do you like it?”

She chewed a bite of chicken. “Yeah, I do. I like have a flexible schedule, and not being tied to one place.”

I loved the way she was so thoughtful before she spoke.

“I started doing it when my kids were young. I had a full-time job at the hospital before I got pregnant, but it was too hard to keep a regular schedule when my oldest was a baby, so I made the change. Travel nursing was the perfect gig because if I needed to take the kids to an appointment or they were off school, I was free to decline an assignment and be with them instead.”

“How old are your kids?” I asked. I had a sudden flash of fear. I hoped she wasn’t married. She wasn’t wearing a ring but that was probably normal for people who needed to wear gloves.

“Christina, my oldest, is twenty-eight, and my son Rob is twenty-five.”

“Do they live nearby?”

“Yeah, they both live within a half hour of here.”

“And their father?” I couldn’t resist asking.

“Last I heard my ex-husband was living in Texas, but I’m not really sure.”

At my questioning look she added, “He isn’t in touch with his kids anymore.” A flash of pain crossed her face, telling me that there was more to the story.

I shook my head. "I can't imagine not being around Susannah. We've always been close, but more so since her mom died."

"Is she your only child?"

"Yeah, we only wanted one."

Emma stood up and walked closer to the bed. "I'm going to need you to eat more of your lunch so you can take another pain pill."

"I don't want another pill," I protested. "I just had one four hours ago."

"Too bad, you're going to take one anyway. Now eat up." The bossy tone was back, making me glad for the coverage of the blanket in my lap.

I dutifully picked up my fork and began eating again. Emma gave me one of her sunshiney smiles and I resolved to do whatever I could to make her smile like that for the rest of her life.

After she took my empty plate, Emma returned with a fresh bottle of water. She handed me two pills and watched carefully as I swallowed them, as if she was afraid that I'd hide them in my cheek or something. Stubborn woman.

"How long do you think my recovery is going to be?" I asked. Since I'd skipped out early from the hospital, I didn't really know what would happen next.

"Since your appendectomy was done laparoscopically, you're probably looking at one to three weeks to fully recover."

"I'll do it in one," I said decisively. I liked having a goal.

She laughed. "It's not a contest. Besides, you'll probably feel significantly better in two or three days. Then you'll just need to take it easy for a couple of weeks while you finish healing."

"So I've got you here for a couple of days?"

Emma nodded. "My assignment is for three days including today, with an option to extend if you have any setbacks. With a patient in good health like you, I don't expect that you'll have any complications."

"Then you'll be off to your next assignment?" I asked.

"Yep."

"Do you ever visit your old patients?"

"Not usually, although some people request me to come back if they develop another issue."

"I'm going to need you to come back. I want to see you again, Emma."

She laughed, but I noticed a slight flush of pink climbing up her cheeks. "I thought you were going to be fully recovered in one week?"

"Oh, I will. I'd like to see you again, but not as a patient. I want to go on a date with you."

"Wyatt...," she started.

I interrupted her. "I know what you're going to say. You can't date patients. I'm under the influence of pain meds. I'm going to be honest Emma, I don't care about any of that. I feel something between us, something big, and it's not the narcotics."

"Wyatt...," she started again, looking conflicted.

I held up my hand. "Don't answer me now. I just wanted to put out my intentions. When you are no longer my nurse, Emma Edwards, I plan to take you out and get to know you better."

"I don't think that's a good idea," she prevaricated. I could see the conflict in her eyes, and by the way she was twisting her hands together nervously.

I hadn't gotten as far as I had in the business world without learning the benefit of taking a risk. This felt like the most important risk I'd ever taken.

"Are you saying you don't feel it too?" I asked. "The connection between us?"

She stared at me for a long time before admitting, "I do feel...an attraction for you, but we come from very different worlds, and we are meeting under unusual circumstances. When you're feeling better, you'll come to your senses and realize you're confusing gratitude for my help with something else."

"I'm not confused Emma, and once I'm able to walk around again, I'll prove it to you. We belong together, and I can't wait to kiss every inch of your delectable body."

Emma

My panties were immediately damp. A man hadn't made me wet just by his words in about a million years. Maybe ever. His words were crazy, but something deep inside me wanted to believe Wyatt.

I'd had many patients over the years, male and female, who had flirted with me. But none had seemed as serious as Wyatt. And none had ever tempted me like he did.

"Let's just get you well," I prevaricated as I watched his eyelids get heavy. Good, the pain meds were kicking in. You could always the people who didn't take pills very often; the narcotics usually would hit them fast and hard.

"Damn pills," I heard him grumble sleepily as he leaned his head back on the pillow. "I wasn't done talking."

The rest of the day passed quickly. Wyatt slept off and on most of the day, which was typical for someone in his condition. When he was awake we chatted easily, getting to know each other in a way I didn't usually do with patients. When he napped I read about the growing love been curvy Natasha and her billionaire boss.

As promised, Susannah bustled in just after seven, laden down with bags of Thai take-out that looked like enough to feed a huge group. Both father and daughter tried to insist that I stay for dinner, but I demurred.

My shift was over and despite our frank conversations earlier, I was hesitant to blur the lines between us too much more. At least not while Wyatt was my patient. I had an ethical code that I'd been following for my almost thirty-year career, and I wasn't going to mess it up now.

I bid goodnight to Wyatt and Susannah, giving her instructions for his care, then I hurried home to make my own dinner. If I fantasized about Wyatt later that night alone in my bedroom well, that was between me and my vibrator.

I spent the next two days working at Wyatt's house during the day while Susannah worked at her own job. Apparently she was some kind of a social worker, and it was hard for her to take time off at the last minute. I went over to the house around eight in the morning and stayed with Wyatt until his daughter returned between six and seven. I learned that Susannah had her own house, but she'd informed her father that she was staying with him for a few days until she was convinced he was well enough to stay on his own.

The daughter was just as stubborn as her father, I thought ruefully.

Partway through the second day, at his insistence I switched Wyatt from his narcotics to ibuprofen. Due to the opioid epidemic, we tried to wean patients off the high octane meds as quickly as possible. However, Wyatt was one of those "grin and bear it" patients who was resistant to any medication, regardless of how much they needed meds to heal. I watched him carefully after the ibuprofen to make sure his pain didn't increase too much.

Over my next two days at Wyatt's house, he and I had long and increasingly personal conversations. I rarely talked about myself with patients, but this felt different. Throughout our time together we'd talked about everything: our childhoods, our marriages, our kids, our careers, and our likes and dislikes. I half suspected that part of Wyatt's resistance to taking pain medication was his desire to stay awake and talk to me. Or maybe that was just wishful thinking..

By the third day Wyatt felt comfortable enough with me to share the painful story of his wife's illness and subsequent death. They had started dating their freshman year in college, and other than a couple of brief periods when they broke up, they'd been together most of his adult life.

"Honestly, I got really depressed after she passed, although I didn't admit that to myself until after I came out of it," he explained. "Our passion had faded over the years, but we were still each other's best friends. We worked together on the business as well as sharing a life together. I tried to be strong for Susannah, and some days that's the only thing that got me out of bed."

Despite our obvious differences, we had a lot in common. Wyatt was easy to talk to. He was a thoughtful and attentive listener, and I enjoyed learning more about him. He seemed to feel the same way about me. In fact, he was quite skilled at getting me to talk about myself. After three days together I felt like we knew each other better than I knew some of my best friends.

I knew that Wyatt was hoping that I would stay and work with him for a few more days, but I couldn't justify continuing to recommend nursing care for him when he was recovering so quickly. Laparoscopic surgery had a significantly shorter recovery time compared to a full incision surgery, and Wyatt was healthy and strong going in. He'd come far in three days. His strength was coming back, and his incisions were healing nicely.

Wyatt was forthcoming about his interest in me. He wasn't smarmy about it, but he made no effort to hide his attraction to me. The more time I spent with him, the harder it was to deny my feelings for him. I tried to keep everything professional, but it was increasingly difficult with his hot gaze, the personal conversations, and all the "accidental" touches between us. It sounded crazy, but after only three days together, I was falling for him. I just hoped I wasn't setting myself up for disappointment; God knows I'd done that in several relationships over the course of my life.

At the end of our third day together, Wyatt asked for my phone number. I was leaning over him, having just finished replacing his bandages, and he placed his hand over my gloved fingers. I felt a thrill of excitement.

"I'd like your phone number please, Emma, so I can ask you out for a date properly once you're officially not my nurse."

I met his eyes. This seemed like a bad idea, but right now I couldn't remember why. Oh yeah, if he didn't call, it would break my heart. Or if he did call and we dated and it didn't work out, it would break my heart. Stupid heart, it was way too invested already.

I opened my mouth to argue, but Wyatt wrapped his hand around the back of my neck and pulled me towards him. He moved slowly but with intent, and pulling away didn't even enter my mind.

The moment our lips touched my entire body came alive. Wyatt's lips were soft and firm and as much as I wanted to lick my way inside his mouth, I was still on the clock. I had professional ethics to uphold. As if sensing my hesitance, he pulled away without trying to deepen the kiss. It was the right thing to do, but I was still disappointed.

While I stood there trying to convince myself that leaping onto the bed and riding him until we were both satisfied was a bad idea, Wyatt leaned over and grabbed his phone off the nightstand. Pressing in the code, he handed it to me.

"There you go. Put yourself in my contacts."

I arched my eyebrow at his bossy tone, and he gave me a rueful grin. "Please."

That was one of the things I liked about Wyatt: he was a big old marshmallow under that grumpy exterior.

I opened up the phone app and input my number, then texted myself so I could have his number as well. Placing the phone back on the nightstand, I moved away before I did something I shouldn't.

We both jumped as we heard Susannah call out from the front of the house. "I'm back!"

I moved away and began gathering up my supplies. I greeted Susannah with a smile as she came into the room.

"How's our patient today, Nurse Emma?" she asked.

I gave her a smile. She was a good daughter. Wyatt and his wife had done a great job raising her. I knew that Wyatt was hoping that she would find someone and get married now that she had turned thirty. Unfortunately, she seemed determined to stay single.

"He's doing great, healing up nicely. He should be fine to move around on his own, as long as he's careful with his stitches." I turned to my patient. "If you get any new redness in those incisions, anything starts oozing, or you experience severe pain you need to call your doctor right away. Don't mess around, do you hear me?"

His eyes darkened the way they always did when I bossed him around. I think he liked it. "Thanks Emma, I'll reach out to you soon."

Ignoring Susannah's curious look I grabbed my bag, said a quick goodbye, and hurried from the room. As I let myself out, I wondered if I'd ever return to this gorgeous house or see its equally gorgeous owner again.

As I drove away from Wyatt's sprawling mansion my phone buzzed with a text, making my pulse skyrocket. I tried to hide my disappointment when the robotic voice of Siri announced that the text was just my boss letting me know she had a new assignment for me.

Wyatt

"So Dad...what's going on with you and our sweet Nurse Emma?"

"Nothing," I lied.

I couldn't believe it when I felt my face heat up with a blush. My daughter's satisfied smirk confirmed that she'd noticed.

"I think you two liiiiike each other, dontcha?" she said in a sing-song voice.

"Shut up," I mumbled grumpily.

Susannah plopped herself at the foot of my bed, her expression turning serious.

"Dad, it's obvious you two really like each other. There's a definite vibe between you two that even I can feel, and I think it's great. Emma seems awesome. Besides, Mom's been gone for a long time, and she would have never wanted you to be alone like this."

"Actually, when your mother first got diagnosed with cancer she told me that if I ever dated another woman after she died she would come back from the dead just to kick my ass."

My daughter laughed. "I'm sure she was teasing you, Dad. You know how she was."

It was true. My wife had always been the funny one, while I played straight man. One of the reasons why we'd been so good together was her ability to lighten me up. I'd grown significantly more grumpy since she'd died, or at least that's what I'd heard from my employees. Well, and my friends and family too.

"Seriously, you like her though, right?" Susannah tossed her long hair over her shoulder. It was thick and dark brown, the same way mine had been before I'd started going grey ten years ago.

"She's it for me," I confided. "I'm going to marry that woman."

The blue eyes that she'd gotten from her mother widened in surprise.

"I come from a long line of men who know their soulmate the minute they see them," I explained. "My father and grandfather were the same way."

"And Mom?"

"I loved her deeply, but it never felt like this," I explained. "We were best friends who fell in love and got married. I loved being married to her, and I think she felt the same way, but it was also very comfortable. There was never this intense connection like I feel with Emma."

Susannah leaned back on her hands, her expression stunned. "Wow. OK. How does Emma feel about all this?"

"I think she's going to take a little convincing. She seems pretty sure that I only think that I'm interested in her because I feel grateful for her helping me. Also, she seems pretty hung up on what she calls our economic differences."

"Really?"

"Yeah, she gave me shit about living in what she calls 'an obscenely huge McMansion' all alone. She also quizzed me about whether I'm giving back to the community and helping the less fortunate."

"A woman who's not impressed by your money? That's a new one," she said wryly.

Women hit on me all the time, even back when I was married, but I only had to look in their eyes to see that they were just money hungry. There was no real interest in me as a person.

"Honesty, I get the impression that my wealth is a strike against me with her."

Susannah nodded approvingly. "When are you going to see her again?"

"I'm going to reach out tomorrow and set something up. Hopefully. She might need some more convincing. She never gave me a straight answer about going out."

I had my doubts, wondering if once Emma was away from me she'd talk herself out of giving me a shot.

Susannah stood up and dropped a kiss on my cheek. "I wish you luck Dad. I think Emma will be good for you. She seems like a cool chick."

I laughed at her phrasing and changed the subject. "What did you bring me for dinner, kid?"

Later that night Susannah finally left to go back to her own house, reassured that I was feeling better, and I gave into my impulses and texted Emma.

Wyatt: *I understand that the rule is I'm supposed to wait three days to contact you after getting your number, but I've never been much for the rules.*

Emma: *Hey, how are you feeling?*

Wyatt: *Terrible.*

Emma: *What's wrong?*

Wyatt: *My favorite nurse is gone.*

Emma: *Haha. [laughing emoji]. You're still feeling OK then?*

Wyatt: *I'm feeling good, almost like new.*

Emma: *Really? That's quite a recovery you've had in the last few hours.*

Wyatt: *Can we have dinner tomorrow?*

Emma: *You're supposed to stay in bed for the rest of the week, remember? Don't make me sic your daughter on you.*

Wyatt: *Please. Anything but that. I finally just convinced her to go back to her own damn house and quit being a mother hen around me.*

Emma: *It's sweet that she wants to take care of you. You have a good daughter.*

Wyatt: *I do. Back to our date tomorrow. We don't have to go out for dinner. We can just eat dinner in bed. Naked.*

Emma: *OMG. You're ridiculous.*

Wyatt: *But incredibly charming and handsome too, right?*

Emma: *I'm taking the 5th on that one.*

Wyatt: *So, about our first official date, how about steak? Or seafood? Italian? Greek? French? Thai?*

Emma: *Before you run out of cuisines to mention I'd like to remind you that I'm really not supposed to date patients.*

Wyatt: *Good thing I'm not your patient anymore. We've already paid the bill. Our business relationship is officially over, which means you can have dinner with me tomorrow with a clear conscience.*

Emma: *Even if I thought this was a good idea, which I don't, I can't do it tomorrow. I have a twelve hour at the hospital tomorrow, and then the same shift on Friday. I'm like a zombie after working that long.*

Wyatt: *How about Saturday night? I can take you to this steak place downtown. Everyone loves it.*

Emma: *You're not supposed to be driving until you're healed and off your pain meds.*

Wyatt: *I'm pretty much healed now. And for the record, I haven't taken any pills since you bullied me into taking one this morning. I haven't even had ibuprofen.*

Emma: *I never bullied you!*

Wyatt: *Yeah you did. You're all steely resolve under that sunshine exterior. But anyway, you don't need to worry about me driving. I have a car service I use.*

Emma: *Of course you do. [eye rolling emoji] This isn't New York City you know. It's easy to get around in this town.*

Wyatt: *It's way more fun to be a passenger, plus you don't have to worry about finding parking. Give me your address. We'll pick you up Saturday at six.*

Emma: *You're a little pushy.*

Wyatt: *Here's the thing about me: when I see something I want, I go for it. I like you. And I think you like me too.*

Emma: ...

Wyatt: *Let's just start with dinner. We can save the naked part for later.*

Emma: *Fine. I'll see you Saturday.*

Wyatt: *That's just the level of enthusiasm I was hoping for. You're going to keep me on my toes, aren't you?*

Emma: *You have no idea, mister. Good night.*
Wyatt: *Good night sweetheart. I'll talk to you tomorrow.*

Emma

It had been a while since I'd gone on a date, and honestly I was a nervous wreck. Maybe because I'd never had such strong feelings about a date before. There was something about Wyatt that made me feel like a girl again.

I couldn't decide what to wear and after dithering for most of the day, I finally called Evie to come over and help. Fortunately, she was not working at the store, so she was able to come right over.

"OK, how bad is it?" she asked as she charged in and headed for my bedroom.

"What?"

"Your wardrobe? Do you have anything decent to wear?"

"Maybe? I can't decide, that's why I called you."

Evie headed towards the closet, flipping through my clothes. "Oh my God, it's really slim pickings in here. You really need to go clothes shopping."

"For what? I rarely go anywhere besides work, and I get to wear scrubs every day."

She rolled her eyes and pulled out a black maxi dress. "How about this? We can dress it up with a scarf." Her tone was dubious.

Seeing my lack of enthusiasm, she went back inside the closet and returned with a dark pink wrap dress I didn't even know I had anymore. Small white flowers with green leaves made a tasteful pattern against the dark pink fabric.

"Wear this with those black knee high boots you have."

I took off my clothes, but Evie stopped me as I started to pull on the dress. "Wait, you're not going to wear that ratty old underwear on your date, are you?"

I looked down at my plain blue cotton bikinis and matching bra in confusion.

"What's wrong with them? They match, and they're not ripped. No one's going to see my underwear anyway."

She shook her head, her expression clearly conveying that I was a lost cause. "You've got to have something cuter in here somewhere. You can't project sexy confidence in old cotton panties, Emma. I had no idea you were so clueless."

"I haven't dated in a while," I reminded her as I searched through my underwear drawer for a better option. "I haven't had a reason to buy impractical underwear."

"You mean you haven't dated anyone you actually like in a while," she corrected.

She was right. Ever since my divorce I'd stuck to dating nice, safe men with low expectations.

"It doesn't matter, I'm not planning on sleeping with Wyatt tonight."

I didn't share that I'd taken extra time to shave my legs and groom myself "down there".

"Planning and doing are two different things," Evie said in a serious voice, as if she was imparting some deep wisdom.

"Ah hah!" I turned around and waved a pair of red lace panties that still had the tags on and the matching bra that had been on top of it way in the back of the drawer. "How about these?"

Evie took them from my hand, examining them carefully as if the future of the free world depended on my choice of underwear.

"These are perfect," she finally pronounced. "Very sexy."

She helped me fix my hair until it fell into loose waves down just past my shoulders, then I dug out my mascara and a tube of lipstick to add a bit of color to my face. I'd never worn a lot of make-up, even when I was young, but I did appreciate a touch of red on my lips.

"You look sexy as hell," Evie told me, giving me a hug. "Have fun and try not to overthink this."

"I'll try," I promised, returning the hug. "I'll call you tomorrow, OK? Thanks for your help."

I headed outside just before six, my purse on my shoulder and a light jacket in my arms, as I waited for Wyatt on the porch. I loved my little house, but it wasn't nearly as nice as Wyatt's giant mansion.

A black town car pulled up in front of the house, looking out of place in front of the modest homes in my middle class neighborhood. I knew it was Wyatt even before he stepped out of the car. He looked delicious in a black suit and silver dress shirt that was open at the neck.

"You look beautiful," he breathed as I walked towards the car. I shivered as his eyes roamed appreciatively up my body. "I've never seen your hair down before."

"I usually keep it up for work," I told him. "You look pretty nice yourself."

He gave me one of his rare smiles and enveloped me in a tight hug. I relaxed into his embrace, inhaling the spicy scent of his cologne, thinking that it probably cost more than my car.

"Shall we?"

Wyatt took my hand and led me to the town car. I slid in, being careful not to accidentally open the wrap skirt, and greeted the driver, who introduced himself as Ed.

We got buckled up and Ed drove towards downtown while Wyatt and I talked softly in the backseat. Sitting this close to him, my entire body was vibrating with awareness. I could feel my heart rate picking up. I hadn't felt like this in a long time, this sense of being nervous, excited, and full of anticipation all at the same time. It was a heady feeling.

"How are you feeling?" I asked, breaking the silence. "Any pain?"

We'd talked via text several times a day since I left his place Wednesday night, but I still felt like I'd missed him, which was totally weird since I'd seen him three days ago. How was it possible that I'd gotten so attached to Wyatt in less than a week?

"Right as rain," he told me. I figured he was exaggerating but didn't push the issue. I'd make him show me his incisions later.

Ed pulled the car up in front of a trendy steakhouse that I'd heard about on social media but never would have come to, given the exorbitant prices they reportedly charged. It was the kind of place that the rich people who had weekend houses on the coast liked to frequent. Several fancy looking people in designer clothes mingled in front of the restaurant, exuding money and privilege. I didn't like to stereotype people based on appearance, but if I did I would have pegged these people as insufferable snobs. They just had that air about them.

I put my hand on Wyatt's arm as he opened the car door.

"Wyatt, this place looks a little too fancy for me."

He looked back at me in surprise. I wondered if the other women he dated liked going to places like this. I'd guess they did.

"Can we go someplace more normal? I hate to be a bother, but I'm not going to be comfortable in a snooty place like this."

Actually, that wasn't exactly true. I didn't mind being a bother. I'd promised myself after my divorce that I was not going to spend even one more day of my life subjugating my feelings for someone else's comfort. But that was a bit much to explain on our first real date.

"Sure honey, we can go anywhere you like. Do you have a place in mind?"

I felt a thrill at the endearment. Leaning forward I said, "Ed do you mind taking us to the wharf? I'll give you directions when we get closer."

"Yes ma'am," he said as he pulled away from the curb.

Ten minutes later we arrived at a nondescript restaurant two blocks away from the Promenade that ran along the coastline. It was the kind of place that catered to both visiting tourists and local residents.

"Dawn's?" Wyatt asked curiously as he looked at the building. "I've never heard of this place. Do we need a reservation?"

I grabbed his hand to lead him towards the door. "One of my best friends owns this place," I explained. "She'll fit us in."

The hostess greeted me warmly. She was another member of our Boozy Book Club. "Emma! Nice to see you." She gave me a big hug before grabbing some menus.

"How are you enjoying this month's book?" she asked as she led us to a table near the window.

"It's better than I expected," I answered honestly. "I can't wait to talk about it with the group at the next meeting."

"That billionaire sounds hot as hell, and the things he does with Natasha, oh my God." She fanned herself with the menus. I laughed at her obvious infatuation with the fictional characters.

"Scott will be over in a minute to take your order. Enjoy your meal."

"Billionaire?" Wyatt asked curiously.

I felt a flush on my face. "I'm in a book club with a bunch of other women," I explained. "It's at my friend Evie's bookstore, Boozy Books."

He nodded. "Oh yeah, I've been there."

"This month we're reading this romance book about a billionaire who falls for his much younger secretary."

"That's not cliché at all," he said drily. I laughed.

"I like this place," he said.

I looked around and tried to see it from his perspective. It was a simple restaurant, the interior decorated to look like the inside of a ship. The walls and floor were all comprised of dark wood plank, with tables and chairs in a matching wood. Fish and fishing paraphernalia on the walls gave a nod to the fishermen who worked nearby on the docks. Candles flickered in mason jars, giving the space a romantic ambiance. During the day, the large windows made the place seem bright and airy.

It was pretty quiet, with most of the tables occupied by couples and a handful of families. Dawn had done a great job with this place. It was clean and comfortable, but still nicer than most restaurants in the neighborhood.

As if I conjured her, my friend Dawn came rushing over to our table.

"Emma, sweetie!" She pulled me into a hug, then pulled away to check out my companion with a curious smile. "Who do we have here?"

"Dawn, this is my date Wyatt. Wyatt, my friend and the owner of this establishment, Dawn Anderson."

Wyatt shook her hand while she sized him up, her sharp eyes no doubt taking in the expensive clothing. Her flirty smile told me she liked what she saw. I was surprised to feel a quick flash of jealousy.

"It's nice to meet you Wyatt. Have you been here before?"

"No, this is my first time."

Dawn grabbed both of our menus. "You don't need these. I'll make you two something special."

As she rushed away Wyatt gave me a smile. "Should I be nervous?"

I shook my head. "If Dawn is making something special, you're going to be impressed, believe me. Now how do you feel about sharing a bottle of wine?"

Wyatt

Emma and I chatted easily while we waited for our food to come. Our waiter returned ten minutes later with a tray laden down with food, Emma's friend Dawn right behind him with another tray.

"Wow," I said. "That was fast."

Dawn placed empty plates and wineglasses on the table, then waved a bottle of wine with a stopper in it. "You guys like prosecco? I have an open bottle I can comp you if you're interested. I had to open it for just one glass. I hate it when that happens."

When we both nodded she poured us each a glass of the bubbly wine. She turned towards Emma as she handed her a glass. "It's bubbly and a billionaire," she said laughingly.

Emma rolled her eyes, then shot me a worried glance. "She knew who you were, I didn't tell her."

"Yeah, it was like pulling teeth to get the scoop," Dawn confirmed. "Fortunately, Evie texted me some details while I was in the kitchen."

We watched as the young waiter transferred several plates from the tray he'd brought. Dawn pointed at each plate in turn.

"I brought you a mezza of small plates. Calamari, horseradish steak bites, shrimp linguini, grilled asparagus in lemon, baked whitefish in a dill sauce, bacon wrapped dates, one loaded baked potato split in half, and a field greens salad with shrimp. Enjoy."

"Thanks sweetie," Emma told her. "This all looks fabulous."

Dawn hustled off with a wave. I stared at the food in shock. "Wow."

Emma gave me the sunshiney smile that always made me feel a bit lighter. "She likes to bring whatever she has extras of, but this is impressive, even for Dawn." She picked up her fork. "Shall we dig in?"

I had to admit that this place was way better than the pretentious restaurant I'd originally chosen. Honestly, I wasn't even that fond of the place, but on the rare occasions that I went out to eat for business or a date I usually went there to impress them. People always seemed to expect that someone of my wealth would take them to eat the hottest place in town, but I should have known that Emma wasn't impressed by stuff like that.

"How do you know Dawn?" I asked.

"She and my friend Evie and I all met in a Mommy and Me group a million years ago," she explained. "Our kids were the same age, so we started doing playdates. We developed a nice support group, trading babysitting, talking about the challenges of being working moms, things like that. They're my people."

"What do you mean?" I asked curiously.

"We're each other's chosen family. Evie and Dawn are the people I call when I've got good news or bad news, or my car breaks down and I need a ride somewhere," she explained. "If I needed to hide a body, they wouldn't ask any questions, they'd just come over with a shovel. Best friends like that are rare. We pretty much share everything."

"And will you talk to them about me?"

Her cheeks turned pink. "Maybe."

"Jesus, this is delicious," I said as I tasted the horseradish steak bites. "This makes the other place's steak taste like ground chuck."

She gave me a wink. "Told you so."

We ate until we were too full for another bite. Dawn brought us a to-go box with dessert after we declared that we were too stuffed to eat any more. Emma and I had a brief skirmish over the check, but I was faster with my credit card. Dawn grabbed my Amex Platinum with a laugh and took it away to run the charge. I left her a generous tip, amazed at how inexpensive the bill was given all the food we'd eaten.

When we got outside I called the car service to pick us up, then we walked hand in hand up the street while we waited, looking into the shop windows, and enjoying the fresh air. It felt good to move after eating all that delicious food.

The town car came about fifteen minutes later, and we slid into the backseat. It was the same driver who brought us here.

"Where to, sir?" Ed asked.

I looked at Emma. "Do you want to come over for a while? It's still early."

She hesitated, and I added, "We can have a cup of coffee or a glass of wine. It's such a nice night, I thought we could eat our dessert outside on the deck."

"Sounds great," she said after a beat. I sagged in relief. She seemed to be having a good time, but she wasn't pushy about spending time with me, and that threw me off a bit. I was worried that she wasn't as invested as I was.

Ed got us home quickly, and Emma followed me to the kitchen, watching as I opened a bottle of wine. It felt good to have her in my kitchen, and I couldn't wait to make it permanent. It suddenly occurred to me that I hadn't kissed her yet, other than that peck on the lips the last day she worked here. Determined to correct that oversight, I stalked over to where she was leaning against the counter. Bracketing my hands on the counter on either side of her hips, I stepped close to her. I could smell the sweet floral scent of her shampoo.

"What are you doing?" she asked. I sensed a hint of nervousness in her voice.

"I've been dying to do this since the first time I saw you."

I leaned down and pressed my lips against hers, kissing her softly. Emma's hands came up to my shoulders and I licked along the seam of her lips, silently asking for access. When she parted for me, I thrust my tongue into her mouth, desperate to get a taste of her. She made a little moaning noise as I deepened the kiss.

I lifted one hand to cup the back of her head, holding her in place. Emma's hands moved off my shoulders and down to my waist, encouraging me to come closer. I closed the tiny distance between us, pressing my body fully against the soft curves of hers as we kept kissing each other. My body was throbbing with arousal, and I was already hard.

I grabbed her waist, intending to lift her up onto the counter, but Emma pulled back and slapped my hands away.

"Don't you dare," she chastised me. "You'll rip your stitches!"

My dick twitched at her stern tone.

Placing her hands on the counter on either side of her hips, she bent her knees and boosted herself up on the counter. Opening her legs to make space for me, her skirt lifted high on her legs, giving me a glimpse of her thick but muscular thighs. Emma pointed her finger at me and gave me the "come hither" motion. She looked so sexy that I swear I almost came in my pants.

Sliding between her thighs, I crowded against her and dropped my mouth to her neck, nipping and kissing my way down to her shoulder before returning to claim her lips again.

Emma unbuttoned my shirt and shoved it off my shoulders, baring my chest and digging her fingers into the flesh at the top of my shoulders. She wrapped her legs around my hips, and I pressed against the heat of her center.

We kissed until I couldn't take it anymore. Pulling away, I rasped, "Emma! We either need to stop now or move to the bedroom. Your choice."

She opened her eyes, looking almost dazed as she absorbed my words.

"Do you have condoms?" she asked finally.

My heartrate picked up so much I could feel my pulse in my ears. "Yeah."

She scooted off the counter and grabbed my hand. "Let's do it. But I get to be on top."

Emma

Wyatt led me towards the stairs, moving quickly. It had been a while since I'd been with a man but for some reason, I didn't have that feeling of self-consciousness that I usually experienced when I was about to get naked with someone for the first time.

"Isn't your bedroom downstairs?" I asked in confusion.

"No, I just stayed in the guest room the first few days after surgery so I wouldn't strain myself walking up and down the stairs," he explained. "Susannah insisted."

Wyatt led me to the master bedroom, which took up fully a third of the upper level. His bedroom alone was easily the size of my whole house. The room was warm and comfortable. It was painted in a chocolate brown color with a thick off-white carpeting. On one side of the room there was a stone fireplace that matched the one in the library on the floor below. Pictures were arranged artfully on the mantle. A loveseat and matching chair, both upholstered in a dark brown fabric, had been placed in a semi-circle around the fireplace. Vibrant red and blue pillows and a blue area rug added a pop of color that brightened the space up considerably.

The other side of the room held a ginormous dark wood sleigh bed covered in a dark red comforter. It was angled to face the large windows overlooking the cliff at the back of the property. In the daytime, you'd be able to see the ocean in the distance. I knew this because the kitchen faced the same direction. Tables sat on either side of the bed, each with a reading lamp. A large dresser was pushed into the corner by what I presumed was a closet, and I could see an en-suite bathroom through an open door.

"Wow, this is definitely an upgrade from your tiny little guest room," I joked.

Wyatt moved over to sit on the bed, patting the space next to him. "Get over here."

I glided over and sat next to him, and before I knew what was happening, I was flat on my back with Wyatt balancing on his forearms over the top of me.

"Feeling a little e impatient?" I teased.

"I've wanted you since the moment I laid eyes on you," he told me, his eyes dark and intense. "I don't want to take a chance on you getting away."

He lowered his head and kissed me until we were both breathless. I'd always liked kissing, but never in my life had I been kissed so thoroughly. It was like Wyatt was making love to my mouth.

When we finally separated Wyatt slid down my body, stopping to open the tie of my wrap dress. He spread the fabric open, leaving me in the lacy underwear set that I was suddenly glad Evie had made me wear.

"Beautiful," he breathed.

Unhooking the front clasp of my bra, Wyatt released my heavy breasts from the constricting lace. I gave a sigh of relief. This bra was beautiful, there was no doubt about it, but it was not exactly comfortable.

Wyatt gave me a look I couldn't quite decipher before lowering his head to take one pink nipple into his mouth. He teased around it with his tongue, then added some suction, making me moan as I writhed beneath him. He moved to give the other nipple the same attention while I ran my hands across his broad shoulders.

He continued moving down my body, shifting to one side so he could slide my panties down my legs. Tossing them behind him, Wyatt shifted to lay between my legs. I opened them wider to accommodate his broad shoulders, then he leaned down and licked up the length of my slit.

My hips levitated off the bed as I whined, "Wyatt!"

I'd never been this turned on, this fast. I could feel the blood pooling in my pelvis, and my clit was throbbing even before Wyatt touched it with his rough tongue. Up and down he moved, spreading my arousal as he lapped at my sex.

Wyatt inserted one finger into my channel, and I gasped. Adding another, he began to thrust in and out of me, fucking me with his fingers. My hips flexed to meet his questing fingers. I was already so close.

He clamped his big hands around my hips to hold me still, then took my clit into his mouth. He circled the throbbing bundle of nerves firmly as he continued to pump in and out of me with fingers. I gripped his hair hard enough that he grunted in pain, but he didn't stop his motions.

"Wyatt!" I gasped. "Yes! I'm so close."

He redoubled his efforts until my orgasm crashed over me, coming in waves of sensation. Wyatt continued to pump his fingers and circle my clit until I finally sagged down into the mattress, panting and totally spent. He looked up from between my legs with a dark smile.

"You're beautiful when you come," he whispered roughly.

I pushed myself up to sitting. "Oh yeah? Let's see how you do. Get on your back," I ordered.

"I love it when you get bossy," he grinned. "It's hot."

"You like bossy?" I laughed. "In that case, lose the pants."

Wyatt rolled to standing and unbuckled his leather belt before sliding his zipper down. I helped him draw his pants and briefs down his legs, tossing them on the floor with the rest of the clothes. His erection popped up against his stomach, bobbling as if it had a mind of its own.

I pointed at the pillows, and he settled himself on the bed, hands beneath his head. I took a moment to peruse him, wondering at how strong and fit he was despite being in his fifties. There wasn't an ounce of fat on the man. Unlike me. I worked hard to stay fit, but I was still softer and curvier than I had been in my younger days.

Leaning down over him, I wrapped my lips around the mushroom head of his thick cock and swirled my tongue around the edge. Wyatt groaned and I felt the salty taste of pre-cum.

"I'm not going to last long if you keep doing that, honey."

I released him with a pop. "Where are the condoms?"

He pointed towards the side table. "Top drawer."

I crawled over him to get a condom, purposely rubbing my body against his, then made quick work of rolling a condom down his length. Without a word, I straddled his hips and lowered myself onto his cock in one long, slow movement. I was deliciously full, his thick cock stretching me enough to give a slight bite of pain that quickly turned to pleasure.

"Holy shit," he gasped as our hips met. He paused for a moment.

"Tell me if you feel any pain at your incision," I cautioned.

"My incision?" he said incredulously. "That's literally the last thing on my mind right now."

I laughed and began riding him, lifting slowly until our bodies were almost separated, then pushing back down quickly.

"More," he gasped. His fingers gripped my hips so tightly I wouldn't be surprised to see bruises later.

Lowering my hands to his chest so I had something to push against, I increased my pace, moving roughly up and down. Wyatt bent his knees for leverage and brought his pelvis up to meet mine, stroke for stroke. I was already impossibly close, despite already getting off once already. I couldn't remember the last time I'd had two orgasms in a row. Maybe never.

As if he'd read my mind, Wyatt reached up and pinched one nipple in each hand, firmly rolling them between his fingers. The added pleasure was enough to trigger another orgasm.

"Wyatt!" I wailed as I shuddered and shook before collapsing on top of him with a deep sigh of contentment.

He rolled me over to my back, drawing my feet around his lower back. He plowed into me roughly, and it only took a few pumps before he stiffened over me.

"Emma," he growled. "I'm coming."

I felt the warm spurts of his cum as his orgasm hit, lasting so long I was sure he'd completely filled the condom. He collapsed on top of me, gasping for breath as he rested his head on my shoulder. We lay there not moving for several minutes before Wyatt rolled over to his side with a groan, taking me with him.

"Did I squish you?" he asked. His voice was low and rough.

"Only in the best way," I responded.

He leaned over and kissed me sweetly, before pulling out of me. I felt so empty, missing our connection. Wyatt reached over to the bedside table for a Kleenex, carefully removing the condom and wrapping it in a tissue before rolling back to my side. He lay his head on my shoulder, legs tangling with mine.

We snuggled that way for several long minutes before either of us moved.

"How about that dessert now?" I finally asked.

Wyatt gave me a look that could only be described as filthy. "I might need a few minutes to recover first."

"Actual dessert," I clarified. "I'm somehow hungry again."

Wyatt gave me a smile. "Whatever the lady wants."

Wyatt

Emma and I sat on the deck, drinking wine, and eating the dessert that Dawn had sent home with us. It was a clear, cool night, and we snuggled together under a blanket while we stared out in the direction of the ocean. We couldn't see it in the darkness, but we could hear the waves crashing against the shore below the cliff my house was built on.

The view of the ocean was the main selling point when we bought this house. I'd spent hours staring out at the water, listening to the sound of the surf against the rocks.

Just like everything at dinner, the cheesecake and berry pie Dawn sent us home with was delicious. The woman really was a culinary genius. This town was full of foodies, and I was surprised they hadn't discovered Dawn's restaurant yet. If it had been downtown instead of by the wharf, it probably would be the hottest restaurant in town. From now on, I was going to recommend it to everyone I knew.

"How would you feel about sleeping over?" I asked. I didn't want to freak Emma out by pushing too hard too fast, but I hated the idea of ending our night together. Our lovemaking had been explosive, easily the best I'd ever had, but I was enjoying spending time with her just as much.

"Do you snore?" she asked.

I laughed. "Probably. It's been years since someone slept in the same bed as me though, so I can't say for sure."

Emma studied me carefully, as if she was trying to decide if my offer was genuine. I decided to put my cards on the table.

"We're not kids anymore Emma," I started, taking her small hand in mine.

"Thanks for reminding me," she rejoined, rolling her eyes.

"What I mean is, I'm too old to play games. I like you Emma, and I see a future for us. Together, I mean."

I resisted the urge to tell her that I was already in love with her. I'd fallen for her before she even shoved those pills in my mouth the first day. But I figured that should wait until at least our second date.

"This is happening pretty fast, Wyatt." My impulse to hold back had been spot on.

"I know, but that doesn't mean it's not real. It feels real to me," I told her truthfully. "I'm so attracted to you I've been half hard since the moment I laid eyes on you. But more than that, I enjoy spending time with you Emma. Please tell me that you feel the same."

I would probably die if she told me this was all one-sided.

She turned and studied my face for a long moment. Finally she whispered, "It feels real to me too, Wyatt. I'm not normally impulsive, but something about you makes me want to throw caution to the wind."

"Does that mean you'll stay with me tonight?" I asked, resisting the urge to add "and forever".

"OK but if you snore I might have to put a pillow over your face," she said, lightening the mood. "I've been sleeping alone for a long time, and I'm not used to noise anymore."

I released a breath I didn't even know I was holding.

"Deal."

"One more thing," she added, her voice a little unsure.

"What is it, Sweetheart?"

"I'm in menopause and you're the first guy I've slept with in a couple of years."

"What are you saying?"

"I can't get pregnant, and I get tested every year at my physical, so I know I'm clean. We don't need really need to use condoms, unless you're not sure if you're clean."

My dick immediately rose to attention again.

"I just thought I'd mention it as an option," she continued. "But if you prefer to keep using them, it's no problem though."

"I'm clean," I confirmed with a big smile. "Let's go bareback."

She smacked my chest and giggled. "Gosh, that was so romantic."

We headed back into the house, and I felt a sense of total contentment knowing that my woman was going to spend the night with me. When we got back upstairs Emma insisted on examining my surgery wounds, worried that I'd pulled something during our earlier activities.

After she decreed that my dissolvable stitches were still healing nicely, I got her undressed so we could have another round.

We might be in our fifties, but we were both pretty fit and our recovery time was blessedly short. We made love for the second time, this time slow and easy, and after we'd both had our release, I cuddled Emma into my side until I fell into a deep and restful sleep.

I woke up alone and had a brief flash of panic, thinking that Emma had left me. I headed downstairs in a rush, slowing when the smell of bacon hit my nose. Emma was in the kitchen, dressed only in one of my sweatshirts and a pair of my gym socks. The sweatshirt hit her mid-thigh and slid off one bare shoulder. Her hair was a messy tumble down her back, and I could see the red of beard burn along her jaw. She looked adorable.

"What's happening here?" I asked.

Emma jumped and whirled around. "Oh my gosh, you startled me. I was just making us some breakfast, I hope you don't mind. I'm starving after last night."

I stalked over to her, staring into her eyes. "I would be thrilled to find you in my kitchen every day for the rest of my life."

"Because I made you bacon?"

"No, because of you."

She laughed like I was kidding. Little did she know. I leaned forward and gave her a kiss that left us both breathless. Emma pulled away with a smirk. "Don't make me burn the bacon."

"That would be a disaster." I crossed over to the coffee pot and poured us both a cup. "How do you take your coffee? Cream? Sugar?"

"Black."

Emma plated our breakfast and moved to the table that I'd set up near the sliding glass door. I loved sitting here in the morning drinking my coffee and staring out at the ocean waves below.

"This looks delicious," I told her, eyeing my plate of bacon, eggs, toast, and cut fruit.

We ate in a comfortable silence, each of us lost in our own thoughts. After we'd polished off our food, I loaded the dishes into the dishwasher while Emma wiped off the table. She stopped awkwardly in the doorway.

"I guess I should get going," she said quietly. "I'm sure you have stuff to do today."

I felt a stab of panic at the thought of her leaving.

"What are you doing today? You're not working, right?"

She shook her head. "No, I don't have any jobs today. I was planning to do some laundry, maybe clean up the house a bit."

"How would you feel about going to the Farmer's Market with me?" I asked.

Her eyes lit up with pleasure. "That sounds like a way better idea. I love the Farmer's Market," she responded. "But I would need to go home and change clothes first."

As much as I loved seeing her wearing my clothes, I knew she was right.

"I'll call for a car."

I waited in the car while Emma went into her house to change clothes. She returned ten minutes later, wearing skintight jeans and a chambray shirt over a fitted tank top. With her hair up in a high ponytail and her eyes covered by sunglasses, she could have easily passed for a much younger woman.

We spent the morning strolling hand in hand around the Farmer's Market, completely lost in each other as we made our way through the stands. After stocking up on fresh produce we went back to my house and hung out by the pool, reading until we lost the light. It was a nice, quiet day, full of long conversations interspersed with comfortable silences.

That night as we fell into each other's arms once again, I knew I had to do whatever I could to keep Emma close to me. For the rest of my life.

Emma

The next two weeks passed like a whirlwind. When I wasn't working, I spent every free minute with Wyatt. We'd been together every night, and when we were apart, he was always on my mind. I felt like a teenager with a crush, but I was fairly sure he felt the same way. I didn't want to jinx myself, but things seemed to be going very well between the two of us.

Wyatt was almost the exact opposite of my ex-husband. He was kind and considerate and didn't expect me to wait on him hand and foot. Looking back at my marriage, I couldn't believe I'd put up with my ex for so long. I'd stuck with him until our youngest went to college, then told him I wanted out.

My kids hadn't been surprised when I'd broken the news that we were getting divorced. They could tell that their father and I hadn't been happy in a long time, and it bothered both of them how rude he was to me. It was only after we'd been apart for a while that I'd realized that he wasn't just rude, he was emotionally abusive to both me and our kids. My greatest regret was that I'd stayed married to him for so long.

Unlike my kids, my ex-husband had been shocked when I'd asked for a divorce. To say it was an acrimonious divorce was like saying a hurricane was windy. Given that experience, my jumping all-in with Wyatt after one date was totally out of character for me. But I decided to go with it. I might end up hurt, well, I'd probably end up hurt, but I was determined to have fun with Wyatt while it lasted.

"Do you want to do something tonight?" Wyatt asked.

He looked at me over his iPad, glasses perched at the end of his nose. How could someone be so attractive wearing reading glasses?

We had spent the night at my house, and now we were both having a cozy breakfast in my kitchen before we both headed to work. I'd been pleasantly surprised that Wyatt didn't mind spending time at my house. It was much smaller and less luxurious than his place, but I'd worked hard to make it a welcoming space and he seemed comfortable here.

"No, I can't tonight. It's Boozy Book Club night."

"Ah yes, the billionaire's assistant, huh?"

I rolled my eyes. "It isn't my preferred reading genre, but I have to admit that the book was better than I expected," I told him. "In fact, there was this one scene in the billionaire's office that I wouldn't mind recreating. I just need to pick up a plaid skirt..."

Wyatt growled, making me laugh.

"I'll call you after I get home, OK?"

My shift at the hospital ran longer than I expected that day, so I was the last one to get to book club. Evie and Dawn had saved me a seat between them. Evie poured me a glass of champagne cocktail, our drink of the month, and handed it to me as I slipped into my chair.

"Here's your bubbly," she whispered, "After we're done discussing Natasha's billionaire, we need to hear everything about your new billionaire. I've hardly seen you all month."

The group discussed the book for about an hour, then the discussion wound down.

"It's my turn to choose a book," Evie announced. "Our theme for next month is Martinis and Mysteries, and we're going to be reading 'The Mystery of Cedar Cove'. As always, copies are available for purchase at the check-out area. Enjoy your reading ladies, and as always, thanks for supporting the Boozy Book Club."

Dawn and I helped Evie gather up dirty glasses and napkins as the book club ladies made their way downstairs to buy next month's book. When we were finished, the three of us sat at a table, splitting the rest of the champagne cocktail between us as we caught up. We all lived within walking distance, so we didn't need to worry about driving.

I really loved my girls. Ever since Dawn and Evie and I had met back when we were new mothers participating in Mommy and Me classes we'd been the constant in each other's lives. All three of us had experienced ups and downs over the years, but our kids had grown up together and we were all still very close.

"So, what's up with you and Daddy Warbucks?" Evie asked. "You've been very quiet on our group chat, and this is the first time I've seen you in weeks."

I rolled my eyes. "Well, as you know we went out for the first time a couple of weeks ago."

"And ended up at my restaurant, looking all lovey dovey," Dawn added.

She looked at Evie. "They were adorable together."

"Yes," I said, "And thank you again for a delicious dinner. We both really enjoyed it."

"Your silver fox also left us a jaw dropping gratuity," Dawn told me. "You can bring him by any time."

"I don't care about the dinner," Evie said, waving her hand impatiently. "You know I haven't dated in so long I have cobwebs in my coochie. Get to the hot stuff."

I shot her an exasperated look. "I'm not one to kiss and tell," I said primly. Of course, I rarely had any kisses to tell anyone about...

Dawn and Evie waited me out, twin looks of exasperation on their faces.

"Fine." I relented. "After dinner we went back to Wyatt's place, and one thing led to another..."

"I KNEW you would need that nice underwear," Evie said triumphantly. She looked over at Dawn and added, "She definitely needed my help, you should have seen those ugly granny pants she was planning to wear for her date."

"Do we really want to talk about my underwear?" I asked.

"No, get to the good stuff," Dawn demanded, waving her hand impatiently.

"I spent the night with him."

"How was it?" Evie asked.

I felt myself blush. "It was incredible. Honestly, he's the best lover I've ever had."

Dawn and Evie squealed like teenagers.

"And then what happened?" Dawn asked. "I assume things are going well since you've been MIA."

"They are. We've been together every night since then. And pretty much any other time when we're both not working."

"Did he fly you to Paris for a romantic dinner yet?" Evie asked, her voice sounding dreamy.

I shook my head. "You know I'm not impressed by fancy stuff. In fact, he'd made a reservations at 'La Bergerot' for our first date, but I told him it was too snooty for me. He was cool about it though. Then we went to Dawn's instead."

"The food is better at Dawn's," Evie said in a 'duh' voice.

"Damn straight," Dawn responded. "But thank you for saying it."

"I will say that Wyatt is very down-to-Earth for someone with that kind of money," I told the girls. "Other than his insistence on being chauffeured everywhere anyway. He's a pretty simple guy. He likes to read, hike, cook, stuff like that. He hates rich people stuff like golf or going to the country club."

"Do we even have a country club here?" Dawn asked.

"Apparently there's one in Lewiston," I said, referring to a neighboring town. "I only know that because Wyatt had to go to a business dinner there recently and he was grumbling about it."

"Here's the important question," Dawn asked. "How does he treat you?"

"Good." I ticked off each quality on my fingers. "He's considerate, a good listener, he respects my opinion, he isn't threatened by my independence, and he loves to text me sweet little messages throughout the day. Also, he always makes sure I come before he does."

"The exact opposite of your ex," Dawn pointed out. "That's refreshing."

"You've got a unicorn there," Evie said. "I should know, I've been dating for a very long time. You'd better put a ring on him before some other desperate woman snatches him up."

"We've only known each other for like three weeks," I protested.

"When it's right, it's right," Evie responded. "What are you waiting for?"

"I bet he proposes soon," Dawn added. "I can't wait to be your maid of honor."

"Hey!" Evie protested. "What about me?"

"We can be co-maids of honor," Dawn assured her.

That night as I lay in bed alone I replayed the conversation with my friends. As much as I'd tried to ignore my friends' teasing, their words had really freaked me out.

Things were going really well with Wyatt, and it was starting to make me nervous. I'd been charmed by my ex-husband once upon a time, and then I wasted twenty years of my life being belittled and taken for granted. I'd worked hard after my divorce to ensure that I'd never be dependent on a man again, yet here I was, spending every free minute with him.

Besides, what did I really know about Wyatt anyway? My feelings for him were all-consuming, but maybe I was being blinded by my hormones. This relationship couldn't possibly be as good as it seemed. What if he turned mean and controlling like my ex had?

As I tossed and turned in my bed, alone in bed for the first time in weeks, I realized that this whole situation with Wyatt was too much, too fast. We'd jumped right into what felt like a serious relationship, acting like we were two teenagers going steady for the first time. It was crazy.

The more I thought about it, the more I was convinced that I needed to put the brakes on my relationship with Wyatt. I needed some space so I could process my feelings. I needed to slow things down before one of us got hurt. Like me.

Wyatt

Emma was pulling away from me. I wasn't sure why, but I could feel it. She'd spent the last two nights at her own place, blaming work, but I suspected it was something else. Her texts had been shorter and less frequent, and I'd spent two full days staring at my phone like a lovesick teen instead of working.

I growled as I closed down a document that I'd been staring at for over an hour. This was ridiculous. We were adults, not teenagers. We needed to talk face to face. I wasn't sure if Emma was on a job today, but I knew she kept her phone off when she was working so it was safe to text her anytime.

Wyatt: *I miss you. Can we have dinner tonight?*

I saw the bubbles, telling me she was composing a response, but then they stopped.

Wyatt: *Is something wrong?*

Emma: *No. Maybe...*

Wyatt: *It feels like you're avoiding me. Please, talk to me. Tell me what's wrong so I can fix it.*

Emma: *It's not you. It's just that this thing between us, it's moving really fast.*

Wyatt: *And that scares you?*

Emma: *Doesn't it scare you? We're a little old to be acting foolish.*

Wyatt: *How is having strong feelings foolish? If you're having doubts, let's talk about them.*

Emma: *I just need some time to think.*

Wyatt: *Can I share something with you?*

Emma: *Of course.*

Wyatt: *I'm falling for you. I wasn't planning to say that in a text, but there you go.*

Emma: *It's too soon.*

Wyatt: *I don't care. I know how I feel. Please, can I see you tonight so we can talk live?*

I watched the bubbles appear and disappear several times before I got a response.

Emma: *OK. How about I come over at six?*

Wyatt: *Sounds great.*

Emma: *I'll bring pizza.*

My doorbell rang a few minutes after six. I sprinted to the door like a man possessed.

"Pizza delivery."

Emma held up a large pizza box. She was wearing a long skirt, her hair loose around her shoulders the way I liked it best. Her eyes were wide and uncertain, and I noticed that she looked tired as if she hadn't been sleeping well. I knew the feeling.

I took the pizza out of her hands and placed it on the table near the front door. I pulled Emma into the house by her wrist and swung the door closed. Backing her up against the door, I crowded close, surrounding her with my body. I put my hands on the door at either side of her head.

Emma's eyes widened as I pressed my pelvis into hers. I'd gotten hard the minute I saw her on the porch. Around her I was as randy as a teenage boy. I laughed at myself for using such an old-fashioned word, but it was true.

"Someone missed you," I whispered, as I ground my cock against her. I felt better now that I was finally close to her again.

She giggled. "You're crazy."

I lowered my head and kissed her deeply, my tongue sliding into the heat of her mouth. As ridiculous as it would sound if I said this aloud, there was something about kissing this woman that felt like coming home. It was like everything inside me settled the minute I knew she was back here in my house with me.

Whatever was bothering her, we would work it out. Together.

I dragged my mouth away from hers, nipping down the side of her neck to the top of her shoulder. I grabbed her flesh between my teeth and bit down, adding suction. I hadn't given a woman a hickey since I was in my teens but somehow I felt a strong urge to mark her as mine. Something about Emma stirred me on a primal level.

She moaned against the onslaught, digging her fingers into my shoulders as I sucked on her neck.

I reached down and slid her maxi skirt up, bunching the material around her waist, then ripped her panties down towards her knees. Emma jiggled her legs a little and they fell to the floor, baring her to me.

I gripped the back of her thighs, boosting her up against the door.

"Put me down," she laughed, as she smacked at my shoulder. "You'll hurt yourself."

Ignoring her, I shifted her a bit higher. "Hold on."

Emma lifted her legs, locking her ankles at the small of my back. Her hands wrapped around my neck as I reached down to unzip my pants. I shoved my pants and briefs down just far enough for my erection to pop out between us. We both groaned as I slid my hand between the folds of Emma's core, pleased to see she was already dripping wet for me.

After three torturous days without her, I couldn't wait. I knew we needed to talk, but for right now, I needed to lose myself in the sweet heat of her body. We both needed this.

Emma gasped loudly as I speared her with my cock, sinking all the way in with one long hard thrust. I paused for a moment while we both caught our breath. When I felt her internal muscles relax around me I looked deep into Emma's eyes and started pounding into her like a man possessed. My pace was fast and hard and all she could do was hold on.

"Yes!" she whispered. "Wyatt. Just like that."

I increased my pace, rattling the door with my hard thrusts. I was already close, but I wanted her to go first. "Touch yourself," I ordered, taking her hand and sliding it down between our bodies. "Make yourself come for me."

Her eyes darkened at the command in my tone, but she complied. Leaning her head back against the door, she pinched and circled her tight bud of nerves. I could feel her sweet pussy quivering and tightening against my cock, milking me as she got closer and closer to her release.

I lowered my head and bit the shell of her ear, nipping the skin between my teeth as I dug my fingertips more deeply into the flesh of her thighs. I'd learned that my Emma liked a bit of pain with her pleasure, and I was glad to provide what she needed.

"Wyatt!"

Emma's voice was scarcely a whisper as she tossed her head from side to side, shaking and shuddering against me with the force of her orgasm. She was still trembling when I gave into my own pleasure, pushing into her in several long thrusts and lowering my head to her shoulder as I released my seed deep in her body.

Neither of us moved for at least two full minutes, unwilling to break the connection. I gradually became aware of the cool air hitting my naked ass and moved back. Emma unlocked her legs, slowly lowering herself to the ground as if she hated to be apart as much as I did. I pulled out of her with a sigh.

"Stay right there, let me get a washcloth."

"I..."

"Stay," I interrupted.

I hurried to the nearby guest bath and wet a washcloth. Wiping off my dick, I tucked it into my pants and walked back to where Emma stood leaning against the front door. She looked a little dazed. I used the washcloth to clean up our shared fluids, then helped her step back into her panties and pull down her skirt.

"Shall we eat before the pizza gets cold?" she asked, avoiding my gaze. "I stopped at Vincente's."

I dropped the cloth on the floor and stepped closer again, putting one hand on each side of her face. I stared at her intently, waiting for her to meet my gaze.

"I love you, Emma."

Her eyes widened. "Wyatt..."

"You don't have to say it back, I just wanted you to know. I fell in love with you the first time I saw you."

"That's impossible," she argued, although I couldn't tell which one of us she was trying to convince.

"Are you saying you don't feel anything for me?" I asked, holding my breath. I knew it couldn't be true, I just wasn't sure if she was ready to admit the feelings that shone so clearly on her face.

Emma shook her head, but I saw the sheen of tears in her eyes before she blinked them away.

"I do have feelings for you, but...I've been fooled by strong emotions before."

"You were hardly more than a girl back then," I argued. "You're a grown woman now, smarter and wise enough to know what's real."

"I'm scared," she whispered.

"Well then, I'm just going to keep on showing you how I feel until you accept that this is the real thing." My words were a vow.

I grabbed her hand. "But first, let's start with pizza."

Emma

I followed Wyatt into the kitchen, moving to the cabinets to find plates and napkins. I set the table and opened the pizza box while Wyatt headed to the refrigerator.

"Would you like a Blue Moon, Diet Coke, or a water?" he asked. "Or I could open a bottle of wine if you prefer."

"You've got Blue Moon?" I asked, my eyebrows rising. "I thought you said it tasted like, and I'm quoting you here, piss water."

Wyatt laughed.

"It does, but you like it, so I got it for you when I went grocery shopping the other day, along with the diet coke. I noticed that's what you prefer to drink when we're at your house."

I stopped dead in the middle of the kitchen, staring at him. I couldn't believe he'd noticed that.

"You picked up Blue Moon and Diet Coke?" I asked in shock. "Without me asking you? Because you know I like them?"

His head popped up from behind the refrigerator door like a prairie dog. He cocked his head to the side, trying to interpret my stunned reaction.

It was a small gesture, getting my favorite beverages, yet it meant the world to me. In all the years I was married, my ex had never, not once, noticed my preferences. Even when I asked him to get what I liked on the rare occasions he went to the grocery store, he usually "forgot".

"Yeah," he said slowly. "Did I mess up?"

"No," I whispered. "Not at all."

"Oh, good," he said, relief in his tone. "By the way, I also got some of that brand of mint chocolate chip ice cream you like."

That was the moment that I realized I was in love with Wyatt Simmons.

It wasn't because of his money or his looks, or even all the incredible orgasms he gave me. It was because he was a man who saw me, really saw me, and loved me just the way I was. I loved him because he worried about my needs and desires as much as his own. Wyatt was kind and generous and thoughtful and that's what I'd always wanted in a man. So why was I doubting his feelings? Or my own?

I flew across the kitchen, practically knocking Wyatt over. He stepped back against the refrigerator with the impact. I threw my arms around him, resting my head on his broad shoulder and hugging him tight.

"Um. What's going on?" he asked. "I've never seen someone get so excited about ice cream before." He sounded confused.

"You did something nice for me without me asking," I explained.

"Yeah..." He still looked confused.

"You don't understand. You see me. You pay attention, and you really see me."

I lifted my head and stared into his beautiful eyes. "I love you Wyatt."

I pulled his head down and gave him a long kiss. He was laughing as he lifted his head. "Beer and ice cream get this reaction? What if I bought you a car?"

"Don't you dare!" I scolded.

"Can you tell me again?" he asked. "I just want to make sure I didn't imagine it."

"I love you, Wyatt Simmons."

"I love you too, Emma."

He kissed me until we were both breathless. "Now that we've got that we've both acknowledged our feelings, how about we eat that pizza now?"

He turned to open the refrigerator again. "What do you want to drink?"

"Just a Blue Moon is fine."

He brought two bottles of beer to the table, a Blue Moon for me and an IPA for him, and sat across from me, studying my face.

"What?" I asked.

"What just happened? I'm still a little confused."

"My husband never remembered my birthday, let alone what kind of drink I liked," I explained. "He insisted on trying to get me to eat and drink things I didn't like to make me more 'cultured', but it really was a control thing. He criticized and belittled me every chance he got."

"You ex sounds like a total asshole."

I nodded. "Yeah, he was. It was like that boiling a frog thing. I got so used to him being mean to me and the kids, after a while it seemed totally normal."

"I'm glad you kicked him to the curb," he said. "You deserve someone who will treat you like a queen."

"I don't need to be treated like a queen, I just want to be treated like a person with feelings and needs," I explained. "I want a relationship where we're equals, where we're always there for each other, even when things get messy."

"I want that too," he said, his voice sincere.

"You really mean that, don't you?"

"Of course. I intend to spend the rest of my life showing you that I do."

"I'm sorry I was distant the last few days," I apologized. "I hated being apart, but I was getting nervous that you were too good to be true. I guess I'm just not used to being around someone who is so considerate and thoughtful."

"You forgot handsome and smart," he teased.

I rolled my eyes. "Yeah yeah, no need to inflate that ego of yours."

"Can you say it again?"

"What? That you have a big ego?" I teased.

"No, the part where you love me." His look was intense.

"I already said it twice," I reminded him.

"I'm going to need to hear it at least ten times a day."

I set my slice of pizza down and looked him in the eyes. "I love you."

"I love you too. Do you want to move in with me?"

I laughed. “Let’s not get ahead of ourselves,” I told him. “Let’s just take this day by day and see how it goes.”

“You got it. Now eat your pizza, woman. You’ll need your strength for round two.”

“Will that be followed by round three?” I giggled.

“Maybe after ice cream.”

Epilogue – Emma

Three months later...

"I can't believe you're marrying a billionaire, just like Natasha in that book we read."

"You do remember that Natasha was fictional, right?" I reminded Evie.

She rolled her eyes. "It's just nice to see life imitating art."

"I'm not the only one." I nodded at the shiny engagement ring on her finger, and the tips of her ears turned pink. "You're going to poke someone's eye out with that thing."

"I was going to wait until after the wedding to tell you," she said. "I didn't want to take any attention away from you on your special day."

I smacked her shoulder. "Please, it's not like this is my first wedding."

Despite my best intentions to slow things down with Wyatt, I moved in with him less than a month after we'd admitted that we loved each other. We were together almost every night anyway, and Wyatt's place was certainly bigger than mine, so it made sense for me to be the one who moved.

He'd very nicely offered for us to look for a new place together, not wanting me to feel awkward moving into the house where he'd lived with his wife, but I'd refused. Even though it was way too big for two people, I loved Wyatt's house. There was no beating the sight of the ocean from the back of his house. I didn't mind the pool and hot tub either.

We'd done some redecorating to make Wyatt's house more ours though. We'd repainted some of the rooms and redone some of the floor. Between the redecorating we'd done, and my furniture and belongings interspersed with his, the entire place seemed homier and warmer now, in my opinion.

He'd asked me to marry him the day after I officially moved in. I put him off for a couple of weeks before finally relenting and accepting his proposal.

Wyatt wanted to rent out a place for our wedding and have a big fancy event, but I'd insisted that we just have a simple ceremony in the backyard. We'd kept the guest list small. Dawn's restaurant team was catering the reception, and she and Evie were standing up for me. Susannah and Wyatt's best friend Jake were standing up on his side.

My kids had met Wyatt several times now and they both loved him. Both my daughter and my son had told me more than once how happy they were that I'd finally found a guy who'd treat me right. I couldn't help but wish that they'd both find someone of their own. Maybe someday soon...

There was a knock on the door of the guest room where I was getting ready. Dawn swept in, wearing a garnet dress that hugged every curve. Evie was wearing the same color, but a different style.

"Hubba hubba," I whistled.

Dawn laughed. "If only you were a single man. But have you seen yourself, Ms. Bride? You look fabulous."

I was wearing a fitted ivory dress that hit me just below the knee. I'd found it at a high-end resale shop and fallen in love with it. The waist was fitted, and the bodice was beaded, giving it a glittery look. I'd paired it with plain black pumps, and Evie had threaded little baby roses through my updo. I looked very sophisticated.

Dawn looked at the phone she'd pulled out of her pocket. "You ready to marry the billionaire?" she teased.

"No, but I'm ready to marry Wyatt."

"In that case, let's get this wedding show on the road."

***

Want to know what happens next? Emma's friend Evie falls in love with bossy cop in "Martinis and Mysteries". Be sure to check out book two of the Boozy Book Club series.

Did you like this book? Show the love and leave me a review. Reviews are like puppies, they make you feel happy. And keep reading for a special excerpt from "Until You Came Along", available now.

Special Preview

Until You Came Along by Rose Bak

Jen heard the rumbling from all the way in the kitchen. Wiping her hands on a towel, she walked to the front porch to watch the two large buses drive up the long driveway to the farmhouse. Belching smoke, they idled and came to a stop, one behind the other.

Although it wasn't even 10 a.m. yet, the sun shone brightly in the summer sky, showcasing the dust left in the wake of the parked buses. A bird squawked loudly in the sudden silence as a serious looking young woman scurried out of the first bus, glasses askew, a clipboard gripped in one hand, cellphone in another. Two large mountains of men followed her, hulking shadows.

"Jen Oliver? The band is here. We'll just come in and...." she moved to enter the house, but Jen stood her ground, blocking the door.

"Where are they?" she asked the woman, her tone icy. "And who are you exactly?"

The woman looked flustered for a brief moment before her stern mask fell back down again. She shuffled her cell phone into the hand with the clipboard and stuck out her now-free hand to shake. "I'm Simone. I manage the band."

Jen ignored her hand. "Well, manage them out of those buses. They don't get to send the help out to greet their sister."

Simone looked confused as she dropped her hand back to her side. "They're all sleeping. They had a late night. We'll just come in and check...."

"Still up all night and sleeping all day, huh? That's been the same since they were teenagers." Jen shook her head. On the farm they had all been taught the value of hard work – up before dawn, work all day, and early to bed. Somehow those lessons hadn't really stuck with her brothers despite her grandparents' best efforts over the years.

Of course, the boys, as she still thought of them, had been away from the farm for ten years now, chasing fame and fortune as the biggest boy band to hit the charts since N Sync. Like the band that came before them, the Oliver Boys had grown up but continued to enchant teenage girls across the world with their pop tunes.

Simone clearly felt protective of the boys. “They played last night in Wichita you know,” she said sternly. “The show went until almost midnight, then they met the fans and press for hours after.”

“By meet the fans and press do you mean got drunk and partied?” Jen’s tone did little to hide her opinion of the boys and their reputation for debauched partying.

Simone shook her head. “They’ve mostly settled down now. There’s not as much partying as there used to be when they were younger. But they still need to make an effort to meet people, it’s part of the job. Now we'll just come in and...."

Jen shook her head. "Well," she drawled. "When they wake up from their so-called job, you send them on in. The rest of you need to find some other place to bunk. I’m not running a hotel for drunken roadies here.”

A slight movement behind Simone caught Jen’s eyes. One of the giant men flanking Simone shook with repressed laughter, his mouth twisted in a smirk but his face otherwise impassive. Jen looked at him for the first time. He was the size of a small tank, several inches over six feet tall, with impossibly wide shoulders and large biceps. His hair was a dark blond, “dishwater blonde” her grandma would call it, worn military short. He was dressed all in black, and she noticed a gun on the shoulder holster. Jen wondered why he felt he needed a gun out here in the middle of nowhere. She felt him watching her and she raised her eyes to his, a shiver of awareness coursing through her, although she couldn’t make out his eyes behind the dark sunglasses.

“Miss Oliver...” Simone started again.

“Jen”

"OK, then, Jen, we need to do a security sweep before the boys come in. If you could just move aside, we'll get started." Simone nodded decisively.

"A security—-what the hell are you talking about?"

Simone turned to the man who'd been staring at Jen earlier. "This is Nick, he's head of security for the band. He'll be doing a security sweep and assessment with Brian here," she pointed at the second silent man.

"We don't need a security sweep. This place is as safe as it comes. We don't even lock the doors in these parts."

Simone shook her head again, vibrating with irritation and clearly not used to people disobeying her orders. "No way. The boys don't go anywhere without a security check ahead of time. I'm afraid I have to insist."

Jen shot her a look filled with venom, her tone as cold as ice. "You can insist all you like but this is my property. You have no right to it, and neither do the boys. Y'all can just run along now, I'm not having some ginormous strangers poking around my property. Don't make me sic the dogs on you." Simone's mouth dropped open.

This was an empty threat. Jen's three dogs looked mean, but they were incurably friendly. They were just as likely to lick a person to death as bite them. Jen had a sneaking suspicion that if someone tried to kill her the dogs would jump over her body and leave with the killer. But these music people didn't need to know that. If there was one thing Jen hated, it was music people. They were way too self-important and proud.

"Excuse me ma'am," the guy called Nick interrupted.

"Jen," she repeated, a trace of irritation in her tone.

He inclined his head. "Sorry. Jen. As Simone mentioned, I'm head of security for the band. We've had some issues and I would be very appreciative if my team could just poke around for a bit and make sure there's nothing amiss." His tone was deferential and charming, which only heightened Jen's suspicions.

"What kind of issues?"

"I'm afraid I'm not at liberty to discuss that ma—I mean Jen."

"Then I'm afraid I'm not at liberty to grant you access to my property. You step foot off that driveway, and I'll shoot you myself, right after I set the dogs on you. And you," she pointed at Simone, "better make sure no one bothers me again until I see those boys on my porch." She spun on her heel and slammed the door. It was going to be a long day.

***

For more of Jen's story, check out Until You Came Along by Rose Bak. Available at select online retailers.

Other Books by Rose Bak

The Good with Numbers Holiday Romance Series

Love Unmasked

The Thanksgiving Scrooge

Maid for Christmas

Countdown to Love

Valentine's Lottery

Bite-Sized Shifters Paranormal Romance Series

Wolf Doctor

Kat's Dog

Designer Wolf

Wolf Sheriff

Cocktail Wolf

The Oliver Boys Band Contemporary Romance Series

Until You Came Along

Rock Star Teacher

Rock Star Writer

Rock Star Neighbor

Loving the Holidays Contemporary Romance Series

Dating Santa

New Year's Steve

Independence Dave

Holidays with the Shifters Series

Santa's Claws

Bear Humbug

Jingle Bear

Silver Paws

Joy to the Wolf

Lion's Heart

The Diamond Bay Contemporary Romance Series

Brand New Penny

Fresh as a Daisy

Right as Rain

Reunited Series

Together Again

Finding My Baby

Beach Wedding

Non-fiction

What to Do If You Find a Cougar in Your Living Room: Self-Care in an Uncaring World

Catch up with these and other stories coming soon. Join my newsletter for more information[1] *or follow my author page on your favorite retailer.*

1. *https://storyoriginapp.com/giveaways/62ee758e-068f-11eb-904e-c373f6014fe1*

About the Author

Rose Bak has been obsessed with books since she got her first library card at age five. She is a passionate reader with an e-reader bursting with thousands of beloved books.

Although Rose enjoys writing both fiction and nonfiction, romance novels have always been her favorite guilty pleasure, both as a reader and an author. Rose's contemporary romance books focus on strong female characters over thirty-five and the alpha males who love them. Expect a lot of steam, a little bit of snark, and a guaranteed happily ever after.

Rose lives in the Pacific Northwest with her family, and special needs dogs. In addition to writing, she also teaches accessible yoga and loves music. Sadly, she has absolutely no musical talent, so she mostly sings in the shower.

Please sign up for my newsletter[1] *to get a free book and keep up to date on all the Rose Bak romance news.*

1. *https://storyoriginapp.com/giveaways/62ee758e-068f-11eb-904e-c373f6014fe1*

www.ingramcontent.com/pod-product-compliance
Ingram Content Group UK Ltd.
Pitfield, Milton Keynes, MK11 3LW, UK
UKHW041822200726
13854UKWH00001BA/437